W9-BJU-977

Singing Tales of Africa

Singing Tales

# of Africa

Retold by

ADJAI ROBINSON

Illustrated by CHRISTINE PRICE

CHARLES SCRIBNER'S SONS   NEW YORK

Text copyright © 1974 Adjai Robinson
Illustrations copyright © 1974 Christine Price

This book published simultaneously in the
United States of America and in Canada—
Copyright under the Berne Convention

1 3 5 7 9 11 13 15 17 19 MD/C 20 18 16 14 12 10 8 6 4 2

Printed in the United States of America
Library of Congress Catalog Card Number 73–1378
ISBN 0-684-13683-X

CONTENTS

INTRODUCTION

AFRICAN STORIES have been used, since ancient times, as a way of teaching. There are tales which explain how the world began; stories which tell the history of African peoples, the glory and splendor of their heroes and kings; and stories which personify animals, describing their virtues and vices and often adding a moral lesson.

Listening to stories makes learning pleasant and interesting, and the warm, informal atmosphere in which the tales are told binds people together. As we can see in *Singing Tales,* African storytelling gives each listener a chance to take an active part. In all the songs there is either a verse in which the storyteller leads the singing and everybody takes up the chorus, or there is a rhythmic flow of sounds in which the listeners can join in, clapping their hands, swaying their heads and moving their bodies.

So important are song and dance in African storytelling that whole stories are told in song. There are tales too that rightly can be called "action stories." The singing and dancing so completely dominate the tale that but for a few words or short sentences the story *tells itself* in song and bodily motion.

It is little wonder then that the renowned storyteller is one who can invent words, compose songs, and imitate the animals, the people, and the sounds in his story. His listeners, gathered around a fire or under a tree, are lively and alert. They interrupt him with their own witty, complimentary or nonsense remarks, they join in chorus to swell the strains of his verses, and they move to the rhythm of his song.

Singing Tales would not have been possible had not my grandmother, Moke(h), and my mother, Lakosi, taken pains to pass on to me the wealth of their stories. How I remember those times when we would sit together in the evening eating groundnuts and corn—usually roasted, but sometimes boiled, as "Grannie" or "Mama" spun her tales. A few close friends, notably Ann Akpofure and Phoebe Damasio, also helped revive my memory.

Words are inadequate to describe the encouragement I had from my father, who helped Mama translate some of the stories; three of my professors at Columbia University, Dr. Leyland Jacobs, Dr. Arthur Foshay, and Dr. Margaret Lindsey; and Dr. Betty Hunter of Hunter College. Particular mention should be made of Christine Price who assisted with the editing. And finally, I should like to give my special thanks to my wife, Shola, who helped me in all aspects of this work, and to my children who all along were the guinea pigs of my story-telling.

8

Why the Baboon has a Shining Seat

THE SONG IN THE TALE

Chant

SEN CHAIN   SEN CHAIN   SEN CHAIN MA-MA   SEN CHAIN

"Sen chain, sen chain, sen chain,
Mama, sen chain.
Sen chain, sen chain, sen chain,
Mama, sen chain."

"Send chain, send chain, send chain,
Mama, send chain.
Send chain, send chain, send chain,
Mama, send chain."

L ONG AGO BRA BABOON
was a fine handsome animal with thick hair all over his body, from head to tail. He lived in a large village with all the other animals, and the lion was their king.

Now, once upon a time, there was famine in that village. Everyone was hungry. King Lion tried his best to get food for his people, but there was no food to be found. Then he called a meeting of all the animals, young and old.

King Lion had a very loud voice, but on this day he spoke softly and gently. "My people," he said, "I want you all to go home now, but in the middle of the night let the first-born son of every beast in the village meet me here. I promise you that by morning I will be able to get you enough food for a big feast."

The lion had a clever plan, but he kept it secret from the animals. After a lot of arguing they decided to do as he told them.

When the first-born sons of the village gathered together that night, they saw that King Lion was weeping.

"Oh, I am so sad and sorry for you all," he said. "There is no food in the village, and look how thin you are!"

The animals looked at each other, and some of them began to cry too. Bra Dog looked at the lion. He wanted to say that King Lion seemed to be growing fatter and fatter, but Bra Dog could not utter a sound. In the presence of the lion, the animals of the forest lost the power to speak.

"I have talked to the kings of other villages," said the lion, "but they cannot help us. They want us to beg them for food, and we of this village will never beg! Now why do you think *they* have food and *we* have none?"

The first-born sons just stared at him and said nothing.

"I'll tell you why!" said King Lion. "It's because your parents are so greedy. They are too old to go in search of food, but every time you bring home a mouthful to eat, they snatch it! They eat it all!"

Bra Baboon scratched himself and coughed. He knew he had seen King Lion's old wife going out to find food for the lazy king. But Bra Baboon said nothing.

"The Old Ones will make us die of starvation," said the lion. "We must chase them out of the village!"

The rabbit found his voice. "But they have nowhere to go, O King! The beasts who walk on two legs in the other villages do not like our people at all!"

"Well, what are we to do?" said King Lion. "If we let them stay here, we shall all die."

"Never!" cried the gentle white sheep. "Never! I don't want to lose my life for those old beasts!"

"My good friends," said the lion, waving his tail, "I cannot bear to see you lose your lives — any of you — even to save my throne. You are strong and brave and can defend the village against our enemies. The old people can do nothing at all for the village, and they are getting fat while you are slowly dying. You must get rid of them! You must kill them to save yourselves!"

The first-born sons of the village agreed with King Lion. They all went home that night to kill their parents.

But Bra Rabbit was cunning and bold. Instead of killing his old mother, he took her away and hid her in the top of a tall silk-cotton tree. When all the other animals were in the forest looking for food, Bra Rabbit would stand under the tree and sing:

> "Send chain, send chain, send chain,
>   Mama, send chain.
> Send chain, send chain, send chain,
>   Mama, send chain."

Then his mother would let down a long strong rope from the top of the tree. Bra Rabbit would catch hold of it, and she would draw him up, hand over hand, and give him a good meal in the treetop.

The other animals, who had killed the Old Ones, were finding less and less to eat. They soon saw that Bra Rabbit was getting fatter while they were all getting thinner and thinner. So they asked Bra Tortoise and Bra Rat to start watching him.

One day the tortoise and the rat followed him secretly to the edge of the village, and from their hiding place they heard him sing:

"Send chain, send chain, send chain,
Mama, send chain.
"Send chain, send chain, send chain,
Mama, send chain."

Bra Tortoise and Bra Rat saw the rope come down and the rabbit go up into the tree. Then they hurried home and told all the beasts, except King Lion, what they had heard and seen. The animals held a meeting and decided that the next day they would all go up the rope, get a good meal and eat up Bra Rabbit's mother. Bra Baboon was to be the last on the rope because he was big and strong and a good climber.

So the next day, just before the time when Bra Rabbit used to go for his food, all the other beasts gathered on a big flat rock under the cotton tree. Then Bra Frog began to sing in the rabbit's voice:

"Send chain, send chain, send chain,
Mama, send chain.
Send chain, send chain, send chain,
Mama, send chain."

At once Mother Rabbit let down the rope. All the beasts grabbed hold of it. The frog, the tortoise, the rat, the sheep, and every one of them scrambled for a place on the rope, with Bra Baboon clinging on at the bottom. Then Mother Rabbit began to pull. She pulled and she pulled, and she wondered why the rope was so terribly heavy.

Just then Bra Rabbit came running along. He saw all the beasts hanging on his mother's rope and quickly he shouted out:

"Cut chain, cut chain, cut chain,
Mama, cut chain!"

And quickly Bra Rabbit's old mother cut the rope. Bra Baboon sat down with a thump on the rock, and all the animals fell in a heap on top of him. By the time they had picked themselves up, poor Bra Baboon was nearly squashed, and when at last he could stand on his own four feet, he was a different animal.

The beautiful long hair that had covered his seat was left sticking to the rock where he had sat down! His seat was bare and pink and shining.

So Bra Baboon never forgot how the animals had tried to kill the rabbit's mother, for from that day to this the baboon has had a shining seat.

Why there is Death in the World

THE SONGS IN THE TALE

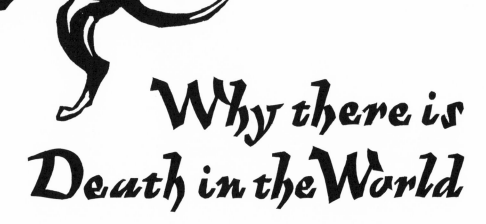

Chant

O - UM   AN-YU   O - UM   A-RU-ON-WU

O - UM   AN-YU   ON-WU SI NA 'CHI

17

"O-um anyu . . . O-um aruonwu."

"O-um death . . . O-um sickness."

"O-um anyu! onwu si na 'chi
O-um aruonwu! onwu si na 'chi!"

"O-um death! from God to man
O-um sickness! from God to man!"

Chant

VU-GU VU-GU VU-GU VU-GU VU-GU VU-GU

LONG, LONG AGO, WHEN GOD made the world, he promised that there would be no death at all. People would grow old, but they would be very wise and strong in their old age.

When God wanted to send this message to the world he chose the dog and the tortoise to be his messengers.

"Go," God said, "and tell all the people that I have created that there will be no sickness and no death on the earth!"

God repeated this message twice. Dog wagged his tail and Tortoise nodded his head.

The tortoise knew that he was very slow, so while Dog was still dancing about and wagging his tail Tortoise started walking to earth.

He repeated God's message at every step he took. As he

raised his left front foot, he said "O-um" and as he put it down he said "Death." Then he dragged his body forward and raised his right front foot saying "O-um" and put it down saying "Sickness." So Tortoise moved slowly and slowly and slowly on, singing:

> "O-um death . . . O-um sickness
> O-um death . . . O-um sickness
> O-um death . . . O-um sickness."

By the time Dog stopped dancing, Tortoise was far ahead, dragging himself slowly and slowly and slowly down to earth. Dog ran after him —

> *Vugu, vugu*
> *Vugu, vugu*
> *Vugu, vugu*

cutting through the wind like a racehorse. When he slowed down, he saw Tortoise far behind, still singing "O-um death . . . O-um sickness."

Tortoise was so far behind that Dog decided to nose about for a bone in a heap of rubbish beside the path. He nosed and he nosed and he nosed and he finally found a bone. He sat down crunching his bone. You could have heard him crunching —

> *Kraun, kraun, kraun, kraun!*

All the time Tortoise was plodding on with his message, "O-um . . . O-um . . . O-um." Dog was still eating when he

saw Tortoise ahead of him again. With the bone in his mouth he started to run —

Vugu, vugu
Vugu, vugu

and before you could wink your eye and say "Mako!" Dog had gone past Tortoise again. Twice he dropped his bone and twice he stopped to grab it from the ground. The third time Tortoise was so far behind that Dog went into the bush, lay down in the cool shade of a tree, and started crunching the bone again. He was munching so loudly that the people on earth could hear him —

Kraun, kraun, kraun, kraun!

Tortoise was still walking. He never stopped. He never gave up. He never forgot his "O-um death ... O-um sickness."

You could see his front feet going up and down, first his left foot, then his right. Every time he would raise his head and bow, raise and bow, and every time he would say:

"O-um death! from God to man
O-um sickness! from God to man
O-um death! from God to man
O-um sickness! from God to man!"

Dog came out of the bush feeling very satisfied and strong and off he ran after the tortoise —

Vugu, vugu, vugu, vugu
Vugu, vugu, vugu, vugu
Vugu, vugu, vugu, vugu
Vugu, vugu, vugu, vugu!

Before you could wink your eye and say "Mako!" he had run past the struggling tortoise. But by now the sun was very hot. Dog was so thirsty he felt as if there were an oven in his throat. Tortoise was far behind again so with a scornful laugh Dog went into the bush to look for a stream and drink some water.

Tortoise still plodded on. At every breath he would repeat his message and make his bow. But his voice was growing weaker and weaker. By the time Dog came out of

the bush, refreshed and strong, he saw Tortoise far ahead with a crowd of people.

Tortoise felt so faint and tired he could only pant his message, the few words he still remembered of God's message to the people. All he could say was:

> "Death . . . sickness,
> God . . . to man."

He went on announcing that God had said there would be death and sickness, death and sickness.

Dog came racing up too late. Tortoise had already delivered his message twice, and no one, not even God, could change it. Poor Dog began to cry. When the people asked him why he was crying, he said that Tortoise's message was wrong. God had said there would be *no* death and *no* sickness in the world.

The people were angry. They knew that Dog had come too late and the message could not be changed. So they told Dog that as long as death and sickness were in the world he would always be found nosing along the roadside looking for food and crunching on old dry bones.

The Stepchild and the Fruit Trees

THE SONG IN THE TALE

1. O-DA — LA ME SO N—DA
2. O-DA — LA MO —O N—DA

SO SO SO N—DA   NWU-NYE NNA MO-O N—DA

NWU-NYE NNA MO-O N—DA ZO-RA O-DA-LA N'

A-FI-A N—DA   LA-CHA LA-CHA LA-CHA N—DA

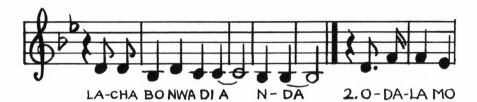

LA-CHA BO NWA DI A   N - DA   2. O - DA-LA MO

"Odala me so	*"My odala!* grow } *repeat*
Nda	Please
So, so, so	Grow, grow, grow
Nda	Please
Nwunye nna mo-o	My father's wife } *repeat*
Nda	Please
Zora odala na afia	Bought *odala* from the market
Nda	Please
Lacha, lacha, lacha	Ate, ate, ate
Nda	Please
Lacha bo nwa di a	Ate and did not give her stepdaughter
Nda."	Please."

"Odala mo	*"My odala!* die } *repeat*
Nda	Please
Mo, mo, mo	Die, die, die
Nda	Please
Nwunye nna mo-o	My father's wife } *repeat*
Nda	Please
Zora odala na afia	Bought *odala* from the market
Nda	Please
Lacha, lacha, lacha	Ate, ate, ate
Nda	Please
Lacha bo nwa di a	Ate and did not give her stepdaughter
Nda	Please
Odala mo."	My *odala!* die."

Once Upon a Time

there lived a family in a village where there were a lot of fruit trees. So many different kinds of fruit trees grew there that in every season, rainy or dry, there was always plenty of fruit in the market to sell. People came to the market from other villages and from the nearby town to buy the good fruit.

The father of the family in this fruit-tree village had four children, all of them girls. But one of the girls, Ijomah, was a stepchild. Her mother had died when Ijomah was twelve years old and her father had married again.

It was then that Ijomah's troubles began. Her stepmother, Nnekeh, never liked her. She only loved her own children and completely neglected Ijomah. Worse than that, she made the girl do all the hard work and did not even give her enough food.

Ijomah's father, Mazo, was too busy with his trade to know what was going on. Even on weekends he was out on business. The few times he was at home Ijomah complained to him in secret, but Mazo never wanted to offend his second wife. Instead of talking the matter over with Nnekeh, he always asked Ijomah to be patient, and once in a while he gave her some money to buy food.

Ijomah's mother had loved to plant flowers. After she died, Ijomah continued to tend the garden. Nnekeh often sent her own children to pick all the brightest and most beautiful flowers, but always once a month Ijomah took roses to her mother's grave. She would have taken the roses more often, but Nnekeh never gave her the chance. At times Ijomah cried over the loss of her mother and over her own sad state. But things never changed.

One day Nnekeh went to the market and bought some red juicy fruit called *odala*. Children love to eat the pink pulpy flesh of the *odala*, and they play games of marbles with the hard black seeds. Of course Nnekeh only gave the fruit to her own children, and Ijomah had none. Ijomah had to be content with the two scanty meals she was given that day. But after her half sisters had eaten their *odala*, Ijomah saw that they had thrown away the seeds. She collected the seeds and planted them in her garden.

When she woke up one day, she found little plants sprouting from the seeds. She was very happy and took great care to make the plants grow up strong and healthy. Early every morning, long before the others stirred from their beds, Ijomah would go to her garden to water the plants. As she watered them she sang this song:

"My *odala!* grow
Please
My *odala!* grow
Please
Grow, grow, grow
Please
My father's wife
Please
Bought *odala* from the market
Please
Ate, ate, ate
Please
Ate and did not give her stepdaughter
Please."

Each morning Ijomah sang her song and watered the *odala* plants she loved so much.

Soon the plants grew into trees, and one day Ijomah saw the first fruit beginning to grow. She was so happy she wanted to dance. She never stopped singing her song.

But when the fruit began to ripen, Nnekeh said the trees belonged to her children, not just to Ijomah. Ijomah was very unhappy. She told Nnekeh that the trees and fruit were hers, but Nnekeh said: "I bought the *odala* in the market, and without them you would have had no trees!"

As soon as the fruit were fully ripe, people came to

Ijomah's garden to buy them. Very many people came because the *odala* were so big and sweet. Ijomah wanted to sell the fruit and have money to buy some of the beautiful things that her stepmother would never allow her to have.

Nnekeh was furiously angry. She raged at Ijomah and refused to let her sell the *odala*. She herself would be the one to sell them. Ijomah was so unhappy she could not sleep that night. Very, very early the following morning, just as the first rays of sunlight appeared, she crept to the garden, stood sadly by the *odala* trees, and started singing:

> "My *odala!* die
> Please
> My *odala!* die
> Please
> Die, die, die
> Please
> My father's wife
> Please
> Bought *odala* from the market
> Please
> Ate, ate, ate
> Please
> Ate and did not give her stepdaughter
> Please
> My *odala!* die."

As she finished the song, the *odala* trees began to shrivel and shrivel until they were all withered up.

When daylight came, the people whom Nnekeh had told about the big juicy fruit went to the garden to buy some. But all that the people found were shriveled trees and withered fruit. Everyone was surprised and annoyed.

Nnekeh was so ashamed she wished the ground would open and swallow her up. She started shouting like an angry general in the army. She knew very well, she said, that her crafty stepdaughter had played a trick on her. Ijomah only laughed and told the villagers that the fruit trees were hers.

"But if Nnekeh wants to," Ijomah said, "she can bring the trees to life again. If the trees are hers, they will obey her! If they belong to me, they will obey me!"

Nnekeh looked at the shriveled trees, but there was nothing she could do. She tried to pounce on Ijomah, but the

people grabbed her and pulled her away. Then they asked
Ijomah whether she could do anything to the trees.

Ijomah smiled and started singing:

> "My *odala!* grow
> Please
> My *odala!* grow
> Please. . . ."

While she sang, the trees began to grow! New green
leaves sprouted from the withered branches, and soon the
trees were loaded with fruit, larger and riper than ever. When
the villagers saw that, they knew the stepmother was wrong.
The fruit belonged to Ijomah, and Nnekeh had been trying
to take them away from her.

So the villagers bought fruit from Ijomah. They bought
and bought. They carried away basketloads of fruit and still
there was more to buy. No one had ever seen so many *odala*
or tasted fruit so fine and sweet. Soon Ijomah was the richest
person in the village. She had money to buy all the things
she wanted, and her stepmother never troubled her again.

Ojumiri and the Giant

THE SONG IN THE TALE

PIAN-GO PIAN-GO PIAN-GO PIAN-GO AYE

GEN-TUL-MAN DON CAM YA TI——DAY FOR

LONG KYAN FOR WA-TA NEAR-ER BUM-PE MON-KI

DRY BONE SO SWEET MON-KI DRY BONE SO SWEET

35

"Piango, piango, piango, aye
  Gentulman don cam ya tiday
  For long kyan, for wata nearer Bumpe
  Monki dry bone so sweet
  Monki dry bone so sweet!"

"Piango, piango, piango, aye
  A gentleman has come here today
  To be boiled in a large can of water
  From the branch of the River Bumpe
  His bone is as sweet as the monkey's dry bone!"

OJUMIRI LIVED IN A bamboo-thatched hut with his mother and his father, Tamba. Ojumiri's father had been a good hunter and a skillful fisherman, but ever since the time when he fell from a coconut tree he had done no active work. Ojumiri and his mother had to earn a living for the family.

The boy cut wood in the bush and sold it to the other people in the village. From the little money he earned his parents paid his school fees and bought the things he needed. Amba, Ojumiri's mother, fried *akara,* made from rice and banana. She sold her *akara* to the farmers who went to work on their farms very early in the morning and to the laundry women beating and scrubbing dirty clothes down by the river.

When he was a strong and active man, Tamba had planted many banana trees, and he also had a big cassava farm. Once in a while people from nearby villages came to buy large hampers of cassava roots for making *garri, foofoo,* and baby porridge flour.

Ojumiri tended his father's farm and helped his mother harvest and preserve the bananas. Once a week he pounded enough "rough rice" for his mother, and early every morning he pounded soft bananas for Amba to mix with rice flour to make her *akara* dough. On Saturday nights Ojumiri would go to the wife of the village palm-wine tapper and buy palm oil for Amba to fry her *akara*. But Amba always said the best palm oil was made by the people who lived on the islands across the river. In the dry season, when the river was low, the islanders could cross safely to the village, and Amba herself would go down to the shore to buy their good red oil.

Ojumiri loved to swim in the river when he was not working. He used to watch and listen to the birds, and he could tell the names of all the birds in the bush. In the evenings he would play and talk with the monkeys in their den, which he had discovered on his way to cut wood, and on moonlit nights he went out to trap crickets in their holes. He had once brought home a little snake, but his mother could not bear the sight of snakes and Amba let it loose. Ojumiri had cried at the loss of his little pet *agbado* and he looked out for another one every time he went to the woods.

One day, Amba asked him to bring her some *tombla tick,* a kind of wood that makes a very hot fire. She was going to boil *akpani* yams for the government men who were building a new road to the next town, and *akpani* needs to be

cooked on a very hot fire to make it soft enough to eat. So Ojumiri set out for the bush, his cutlass in his hand, his ax on his shoulder, and his hunting bag hanging from his neck.

He had a long way to go. *Tombla tick* did not grow in the places where he usually cut wood. He had to go deeper into the bush than ever before. He traveled so far that he wished he had started early in the morning instead of at midday. He was very thirsty. He looked and looked but there was no sign of a stream. He searched and searched but there were no fruit trees, not even a few wild berries to eat to quench his thirst.

Then he came to a clearing dotted with stumps of trees. He stopped short and could not believe what he saw. A hut? A round hut? No! Not in a place so far from any village! Ojumiri never guessed there was a king of the bush who lived all his life in this faraway place.

His heart began to pound. You could have heard it like the *thump-thump* of two mothers pounding new rice.

For what seemed a long time Ojumiri stood fixed, with his eyes bulging. All he could hear was his thumping heart and the sound of the deaf-ear crickets. Then he moved slowly and cautiously toward the hut, as if it were the holy shrine of his ancestors. He tiptoed to the back door and stood there gazing in at the big space of floor around the fireplace.

He was so taken up with what he saw that he did not hear the footsteps of Mbambay. He was frightened out of his wits when he heard a woman's voice say: "Young man, what do you want here?"

If he had not been so thirsty Ojumiri would have dashed away into the bush like a startled bird.

"I — I — I want — " he began, and then he remembered the rule of good manners: always greet your elders politely before you speak with them, especially when the older person is your host. Quickly he lowered his eyes and greeted Mbambay. The tall woman smiled down at him and asked him again what he wanted.

His fears were melting away. "I am very thirsty, Mam," he said. "And I cannot find water to drink. Please give me some water."

"What is your name, young man?" she asked, as she showed him the earthenware water pot.

He told her, and she offered him a plate of food. Ojumiri could not refuse, and the food was good to eat. After he had finished, he washed his hands and the plate. Then, as he started to say goodby, the woman told him of his danger.

"My husband is a giant and the best of all musicians," she said. "He is returning home now. If he meets you on the way, he will catch you and eat you up."

Ojumiri's eyeballs stuck out of his head, and even though his mouth was wide open, he could not utter a sound.

"Believe me, young man," said Mbambay. "What I say is true! You may lose your life before the sun goes down!"

Ojumiri glanced out through the doorway, expecting to see the mighty figure of the giant. "What shall I do, Mam?" he cried. "Please tell me what I must do!"

"Listen to me," said the woman, "and I will tell you a

secret. First of all, I will hide you in the attic until my husband comes in from the farm."

"But won't he find me and catch me?"

"Don't worry! Sit down! You are a good boy and I want to help you."

"But the secret, Mam!" he pleaded. "What is the secret?"

Reluctantly he took the seat she offered him, but you could see he was ready to spring like a leopard.

"Now listen carefully, Ojumiri," she said. "My husband, who is such a fine musician, plays the big *balanji* over there."

Ojumiri looked where she pointed and saw the *balanji* with its row of wooden keys and the two rounded-headed sticks for playing.

"My husband," Mbambay went on, "does not want any other musician to be his rival. When he returns, he will sing a song for you and ask you to play it on the *balanji*. If you play the right tune, he will be so angry that he will eat you up at once! So remember this, Ojumiri: be sure you don't play the right tune!"

And with that warning, Ojumiri was hidden in the attic.

Very soon afterwards, Mbambay's husband came in from his farm. He was such a big giant that his strides shook the ground.

"I smell blood, I smell blood!" he roared as he entered the house. He barely greeted his wife before he started shouting again: "I smell blood!"

Ojumiri quietly and timidly came down from the attic. His knees almost gave way as he stood before the giant.

"What do you want here?" the giant roared.

"I came to drink water, sir," said Ojumiri.

Mbambay's husband gave an evil laugh as he asked the boy to sit down. Meanwhile Mbambay had put a big pot of water on the fire. If Ojumiri played the right tune, the boiling water and the pot would be the end of him.

"Young man, I want you to play this song for me," said the giant. "Play it well, and I shall reward you! Now listen to it carefully:

> "Piango, piango, piango, aye
> Gentulman don cam ya tiday
> For long kyan, for wata nearer Bumpe
> Monki dry bone so sweet
> Monki dry bone so sweet!"

Poor Ojumiri did not like the sound of the words at all, and he trembled while the giant sang the song again:

> "Piango, piango, piango, aye
> A gentleman has come here today
> To be boiled in a large can of water
> From the branch of the River Bumpe
> His bone is as sweet as the monkey's dry bone!"

As the giant sang, he played the tune on the balanji. Then he gave the balanji sticks to Ojumiri to play. Ojumiri was a good balanji player. His two hands wanted to play the right notes. But he remembered the woman's warning. He made himself play such nonsense that the balanji sounded like the chatter of monkeys, the patter of rain, and the clatter of broken pots.

The giant clapped his hands to his ears. "Stop!" he yelled. "You are too stupid ever to be my rival, you young fool! So I'll miss the taste of your good sweet beef!"

He seized the boy by a leg and an arm, threw him out of the doorway, and tossed a bag of money after him. Ojumiri picked up the moneybag and raced away through the bush like an antelope chased by a cheetah. He did not stop running till he came to his village and saw the smoke of his mother's cooking fire.

From that time on, Ojumiri never had to cut wood to sell. Ever since the day when he played the fool before the terrible giant, Ojumiri was rich and happy, and he and his people had plenty of everything.

Ayele and the Flowers

THE SONG IN THE TALE

DA-VI A-YE-LE   NO BU LO MI-DO

BA—BA   NA 'YE-LE YIE YIE MI-DO

BA—BA   NA 'YE-LE   A—YE-LE   NO

BU LO MI-DO BA—BA   NA 'YE-LE

45

"Davi Ayele no bu lo
Mido baba na Ayele
Yie! Yie! Mido baba na Ayele
Ayele no bu lo
Mido baba na Ayele."

"Little Ayele's lost her mother
Say sorry to Ayele
Oh! Oh! Say sorry to Ayele
Little Ayele's lost her mother
Say sorry to Ayele."

AYELE LIVED IN A SMALL
village. She often used to play with the children of her
neighbors.

Sometimes Ayele and her friends would wander into
the hills and watch monkeys. They listened to the birds and
knew many bird songs by heart. When they played on the
river bank, just outside the village, the children used to swim
and mimic the croaking of the many frogs that hid among
the rocks. Ayele liked to catch tiny silver fish in her hands
and take them home to her mother.

But Ayele was happiest when she and the other girls
played on the top of the hill. There they could always find
butterflies and many, many beautiful flowers.

One morning, Ayele and her friends went to the river.
After a shower of rain the day was so clear and bright that
the girls decided to go up the hill and pick flowers. Ayele's
parents had always told her to tell them where she was going,

but she thought that was too much trouble today. What if her mother would not let her go to the hill?

"We shall go and come back so quickly," said Ayele's friends, "that no one will know we have been away!"

As they ran up the side of the hill, they decided to surprise their parents with bunches of flowers. It was May, and there were not only many wildflowers of all colors but crowds of pink and white lilies. Lily time is the time for hunting *ntay*. These tiny insects fly about during the May showers, and if you play outside just after the rain, you can catch hundreds of them as they lose their wings in the bright sunshine. So the girls ran here and there, laughing, skipping, jumping, and chasing *ntay*.

They caught so many *ntay* they forgot that time was passing and the day was nearly done. The sun was dropping low in the sky, and suddenly it was too late to pick flowers to take home. Ayele's heart jumped when she saw the flowers beginning to close for the night, curling up their beautiful colored petals.

Meanwhile, Ayele's mother had gone to the other mothers in the village asking whether they had seen her daughter. But they were asking the same question about their own daughters.

With hearts as heavy as the wood of the *iroko* tree, the mothers set out for the river. Not the slightest trace of the girls was to be seen.

High on the hill Ayele and her friends were afraid. They had wandered so far from the path to the village that they did not know how to get back. Soon it would be dark, and then they would never find the way home. They gathered together and started to cry. But crying would not find the way. They decided to start singing so that if there were any people nearby they might hear the song and come to look for them. This is what they sang:

"Little Ayele's lost her mother
Say sorry to Ayele
Oh! oh! Say sorry to Ayele
Little Ayele's lost her mother
Say sorry to Ayele."

The mothers had gone off in pairs to look for the girls. It was the woman who walked with Ayele's mother who first said she heard singing. Ayele's mother stood still and strained her ears. Then she heard the voices, faint and faraway:

"Little Ayele's lost her mother
Say sorry to Ayele."

Ayele's mother and her companion began to run in the direction of the song. Other mothers too had heard the song and were hurrying the same way. The song was growing louder and louder, leading them on.

"Little Ayele's lost her mother
Say sorry to Ayele."

The sun was almost setting when the mothers reached the hilltop where the children were huddled together. The mothers were breathless, worried, and angry, but when they saw their daughters with drooping shoulders and sad faces, they could not think of scolding them. Mothers and daughters embraced each other. Ayele began to tell her mother the story of the flowers that were never picked, and as they walked home together, they all sang the song that had saved Ayele and her friends.

"Leave it There!"

THE SONGS IN THE TALE

1. AR GO EAT YOU WAN AR GO EAT YOU TWO YOU
2. AR GO CUT YOU TROTE AR GO ROS YOU MA YOU

BRO-DA EN YOU DAD-DIE GO CAN SEE YOU BONE
MAR-MIE EN YOU DAD-DIE GO CAN SEE YOU BONE

"Ar go eat you wan,
 Ar go eat you two.
 You broda en you daddie
 Go can see you bone!"

"I will eat you once.
 I will eat you twice.
 Your brothers and your father
 Will come to see your bones!"

"Ar go cut you trote,
 Ar go ros you ma.
 You marmie en you daddie
 Go can see you bone!"

"I will cut your throat,
 I will roast you up.
 Your mother and your father
 Will come to see your bones!"

MI MAR-MIE AR DA PAN TRO-BUL

MI DAD-DIE MI YAE DA SEE TRAN-GA TIN

MI BRO-DA DEM DO YA UN-AH CAM HEP MI MI

BRO-DA DEM DO YA UN-AH CAM HEP MI

"Mi marmie, ar da pan trobul!
Mi daddie, mi yae da see tranga tin!
Mi broda, dem do ya un-ah cam hep mi!
Mi broda, dem do ya un-ah cam hep mi!"

"My mother, I am in trouble!
My father, my eyes see terrible things!
My brothers, please come and help me!
My brothers, please come and help me!"

THERE LIVED IN A TOWN

a man named Jombo with his wife, Amba, their three sons, and their daughter, Fumikeh.

Jombo worked as a charcoal burner in the forest. Amba was a trader. She used to buy fruit in the villages and sell it in the town market three times a week. The three sons — Ade the eldest, Tunji the middle one, and Modu the youngest — helped their father to cut wood in the forest; and in the villages and the town they sold firewood and sacks of charcoal to make hot fires for cooking.

Many a night the three boys would go with their uncle, Ajagoon, to hunt wild game by the light of a carbide lamp. Sometimes they hunted alone. All three were good hunters but Modu, the youngest, was like an animal of the bush. He loved wrestling, climbing trees, and mimicking the sounds and movements of animals. He could swim like a fish and often went fishing in the sea. He listened to the tales of seamen, and he was a great friend of Daddy Gobeh, the revered witch doctor in the village on the mountain.

Fumikeh, the only girl, loved Modu very much. She did not mind when he frightened her with his leopard tricks. She could even forgive him for teasing when a young farmer named Dele came to visit her.

Dele was a friend of Fumikeh's brothers and he lived in the village of Uncle Ajagoon. Fumikeh first met him when their uncle held a feast to celebrate the birth of a baby boy and she went to the feast with her brothers. Dele was glad to see his three friends again, but Tunji caught him gazing at Fumikeh and making her look bashful and shy.

Dele and Fumikeh soon started seeing each other as often as they could. They had to meet in secret for it was too soon to tell their parents. Modu teased both of them. He would whisper to Fumikeh: "Dele is waiting for you down the road." Fumikeh would run off to meet Dele, only to find no one there. Or Modu would tell Dele that on such-and-such a day Fumikeh would be alone in the house. Her father would be at the charcoal pit and her mother buying fruit in the villages. So Dele would come bouncing into the house — and find the whole family there! Then he would have to pretend he had come to visit the three brothers, and poor Fumikeh would hardly dare to look at him.

Sometimes, instead of staying at home and doing the

cooking, Fumikeh would help her mother in the market. One day, when she was looking after Amba's fruit stall on her own, a richly dressed gentleman came by.

"Hullo," he said. "What have you got for sale?"

Fumikeh had seen him passing several other stalls without even a glance at what they had. She felt quite honored.

"I have good fruits," she said.

"Let me have a shilling's worth of oranges, please!" he said, and he gave her a five-shilling note.

"Your change, please," said Fumikeh, but the rich man, whose name was Orgar, was already on his way. She ran after him with his change.

"Oh, I don't need that chicken-change!" he said. "Use it to get some fruit for yourself, Miss!"

But Fumikeh stood her ground and insisted on giving him the money.

After that, Orgar often came to the market. The next time he saw Fumikeh her mother was with her. He flipped out a five-shilling note, asked for a shilling's worth of oranges, and again walked away without his change. Amba sent Fumikeh running after him with the money.

When she caught up with him, they were out of sight of Amba's stall. Orgar asked Fumikeh her name and where she lived. He told her he was the son of a wealthy family in the town nearby and that his father was going to leave him a lot of property. Not many days after, Orgar paid his first visit to Fumikeh. She and Modu were the only ones at home. Orgar gave her some money, and she was proud to have a rich city person as a friend. All the girls she knew would envy her.

But Orgar was a threat to Dele, who had almost decided to ask Jombo if he might marry Fumikeh. Unlike Dele, Orgar came openly to visit the girl; he did not worry about what her parents thought. Modu showed his resentment against Orgar, but his two brothers kept silent. Fumikeh was happy. It was good to be wooed by two men, so different from each other, but how could she choose between them?

She knew that Orgar came from a town that nobody liked. Many rich people lived there, but they were thought of as greedy. Some had got their riches in devious ways. When the traders counted their money after market day and found false coins, they said the bad money came from Orgar's town.

Dele's village, on the other hand, was well known for its fine fruit and hardworking men. The people were kind and open-hearted. Dele had no money to spend freely as Orgar did, but he always chose the best fruits of his harvest as gifts for Fumikeh and her parents.

One day, when Amba came home tired from the market, she found her daughter alone. No food was ready for the evening meal, for Fumikeh had been off to a friend's house to have her hair plaited. She had put makeup called *tero* on her eyelids and colored her lips and fingernails with the juice of a plant that grew by Amba's window. She was arranging her head-tie in a special way when her mother called her.

Fumikeh was to meet Orgar, and she did not want to keep him waiting. She stamped into her mother's room.

"Mama, please, I can't talk now! Can we wait till tomorrow in the market?"

"The market," said Amba, "is no place for a mother to talk to her child. Fumi, you do not talk to me as you used to —"

"Mama! You know I've hidden nothing from you!"

"Then I shall tell you the truth, child."

"About what?"

"Give me time, Fumi," said Amba. "Allow my words to fall to the ground before you pick them up. It is about this 'big' man who comes to visit you, the one who used to buy from my stall and forget his change. He comes from a town we do not like."

"Yes, Mama," said Fumikeh, "I know."

"It is not a good thing, Fumi, for a man to forget his change."

"He only forgot it twice."

"Yes, my daughter, but that means he wants to use my stall to make *sarra* — to make sacrifice to the bad spirits of his ancestors. That is not a good thing, Fumi."

"Mama, Orgar has told me he wants to talk to you."

"About what?" cried Amba.

"Don't be angry, Mama. I just want to tell you that Dele and Orgar have both said they love me. I don't know what to do —"

"Fumi! Our fathers will not sleep well if you marry anyone from Orgar's town. People will stop buying from me! Even our friends will stop coming to see us!"

"But, Mama, I think I like Orgar. I like him very much — "

"Fumi, I must discuss this with your father. It is too much for me."

That night, when Jombo was smoking his pipe in the cool silence, Amba stepped outside to join him, carrying her little stool. She greeted him softly in the way one greets a person who is sitting down. "Father of Ade, you have done well for sitting."

"Ah, Amba," he said. "You are out late. Aren't you tired?"

"I just wanted to greet you."

"But then you should not be carrying a stool!"

Amba put down the stool and sat on it. There was silence between them until she told him about her talk with Fumikeh. Presently, Ade joined them and Jombo sent him to fetch his sister. She came quickly with Tunji and Modu.

"Fumikeh," said Jombo, "you are my only daughter, and we all want the best for you. Your brother Modu has told me that Dele would like to marry you; your mother has told me the same about Orgar. Dele is a fine young man, and we have known his people for a long time. We do not like the people of Orgar's town.

"Many fathers choose husbands for their daughters, but I will not do that. If I choose a man for you and you are not happy, my dust will not rest in the grave and my soul will cry out. So, Fumikeh, which of these two men do you want to marry?"

Fumikeh begged for a few days to think, but her mind

was soon made up. She wanted to marry Orgar. Amba and
Jombo were not happy, and Fumikeh's brothers were bitterly
disappointed, but no one could persuade the girl to change
her decision.

News went racing around the town and the villages
about Fumikeh's marriage to Orgar. Dele kept out of it
completely. All through the busy time of preparation he
stayed at work on his farm. His best friend, Modu, never
forsook him. The two other brothers were at the wedding,
but Modu could not bring himself to go. He felt too sad for
Dele, too worried about Fumikeh. Something, he was sure,
was very wrong about the wedding.

The great day came at last. For Orgar it was a day of
triumph. You should have seen him! You would have thought
he was king of the earth and the moon! He strutted like a
cock in his finest clothes. Fumikeh was bright and gay and
beautiful. Even Amba tried to look happy. She had worked
hard to prepare a huge feast for the guests, with plenty of
palm wine and all kinds of food — *jollof ress*, *arborbor*, *amala*,
and *eba*. Men, women, and children ate their fill.

It was the custom for the bridegroom to come with some of his friends to take away his wife on the evening of the wedding day. Everyone was surprised when Orgar came alone. He insisted that no relatives or friends should go with them to his home.

Fumikeh felt strange and a little frightened, but she still looked calm and happy.

Then, as she and her husband walked along the road, Orgar's hat fell off. Fumikeh was surprised to see that he did not stop to pick it up and she called his attention to it. All he did was say: "Leave it there! It is there you see it!"

Next his coat fell off, and when his wife spoke to him about it, he cut her off sharply with the same words: "Leave it there! It is there you see it!"

To Fumikeh's horror, as they went on with their journey, everything seemed to be falling off the man. His left hand fell off and then his right hand. He left them lying in the road. At last only his head, body, and feet remained. Fumikeh was too frightened to speak. By the time they reached his house she was so afraid she could hardly move.

Orgar's house was on the edge of the town, in the shade of dark trees. It was a small tumble-down hut with no windows. Inside there were no beds, no stools, not even mats on the floor, and when Orgar pushed open the door of one of the rooms, Fumikeh saw it was full of human bones. She was half dead with fear.

Then Orgar made a great fire outside the hut and placed
an iron rod to heat in the flames. He bound Fumikeh to a
tree, holding the rope in his teeth, and in the darkness of the
night he began to sing:

> "I will eat you once,
> I will eat you twice.
> Your brothers and your father
> Will come to see your bones!
> I will cut your throat,
> I will roast you up.
> Your mother and your father
> Will come to see your bones!"

As Fumikeh listened to his words, she remembered that
her brothers used to go hunting at night. Her throat was as
dry as an empty gourd, but she knew she must try to sing.
Perhaps, somewhere in the forest, her brothers would hear
her voice. So she gathered all her strength and sang:

> "My mother, I am in trouble!
> My father, my eyes see terrible things!
> My brothers, please come and help me!
> My brothers, please come and help me!"

Ade, Tunji, and Modu were deep in the forest when
Modu's sharp ears caught the sound of singing. At first he
took no notice. But still the strange sad music came to him.
He spoke to his brothers. They stopped to listen, then moved
together in the direction of the sound. As they drew nearer,

the doleful wailing grew louder, and they could hear the
words of the song.

> "My mother, I am in trouble!
> My father, my eyes see terrible things!
> My brothers, please come and help me!
> My brothers, please come and help me!"

"It is Fumikeh!" said Modu, and the three brothers ran
through the forest as fast as they could put foot to the
ground. At last they came to Orgar's house.

They saw Fumikeh bound to the tree, and Orgar, the
evil genie with the great head and glowing eyes, standing by
the fire. The iron rod was red-hot in the flames.

When Fumikeh saw Modu in the light of the fire, she
cried out and stopped singing, but Orgar noticed nothing.

"Mother-in-Law, Today is Shake-head Day!"

THE SONG IN THE TALE

MO-DEN-LAW TI-DAY NAR SHAKE ADE DAY

MO-DEN – LAW TI-DAY NAR SHAKE ADE DAY

"Modenlaw, tiday nar Shake ade Day!
Modenlaw, tiday nar Shake ade Day!
Modenlaw, tiday nar Shake ade Day!
Modenlaw, tiday nar Shake ade Day!"

"Mother-in-Law, today is Shake-head Day!
Mother-in-Law, today is Shake-head Day!
Mother-in-Law, today is Shake-head Day!
Mother-in-Law, today is Shake-head Day!"

B RA SPIDER HAD BEEN happily married for several years. He had a wife and ten children. Before he got married he lived alone, doing what he wanted to do and eating all he wanted to eat — and that meant all that he could find.

Bra Spider used to eat so much that by the time he got married he had grown very fat. The other animals used to laugh at Bra Spider. Only the insects and little birds dared not laugh, for fear they would fall victim to his anger and his greed. Although Bra Sprider's body was so fat, he never seemed to feed his legs. They were thin, so very, very thin that the other animals said that if Bra Spider ran on hard ground his legs would break. His head was so very small that when he wore his top hat it slipped down over his head and sat on his shoulders.

But after Bra Spider's wedding all this was changed. He had a wife and ten children to feed.

"You silly woman!" he would say to his wife. "You have twice as many children as you should have!"

"You are the silly one, Bra Spider," his wife retorted. "Who has the children — me or you or us?"

They argued and argued. Bra Spider would accuse his wife of all sorts of things, but he never came out with the real trouble. He was hungry. Ever since his wedding, he had never had enough to eat. When more and more children came, there was less and less food for Bra Spider.

Within a few years of his marriage Bra Spider had grown as thin as your smallest finger. When he walked out with his big top hat on, it slipped down over his poor thin body until all you saw was a hat walking down the road. You had to look twice before you knew it was Bra Spider! The animals wondered what had happened to their old friend with his tiny head, fat body, and spindly legs.

Now Bra Spider's mother-in-law was famous for her cooking and always kept a good store of food. Any time he paid her a visit he could eat and eat until he was full, but he knew if he went too often he would have to take the whole family. Otherwise Mother-in-Law might ask awkward questions. With the family there, Bra Spider would have no chance to eat his fill. He wanted them to believe he was a respectable man. How could he grab food from Mother-in-Law's larder before the eyes of his wife and ten children?

So once in a long while Bra Spider went alone to see his dearest Mother-in-Law. She always told him playfully that his words were as sweet as sugar cane.

"Sure," said Bra Spider to himself. "Sweet, sugary words will bring out plenty of food!"

It was on one of these visits to Mother-in-Law that Bra Spider became the finest dancer in the town.

He had not seen her for a long time, and that day he put on his best clothes, complete with an oversized tuxedo and of course the big top hat. You should have seen Bra Spider go down the road! If the wind had blown strongly, he would have taken flight like a bird and drifted away through the air.

He was going like this:

> *Kunye, kunye,*
> *Kunye, kunye,*
> *Kunye, kunye,*

stepping along with little baby steps. You might have been tempted to hold his hand and sing to him, like a mother who is teaching her child to walk:

> *Tete-o-tete, tete-o-tete,*
> *Tete-o-tete, tete-o-tete!*

When Bra Spider reached the house of his mother-in-law, she welcomed him as though he were her only son who had been gone for years.

"Ah! my pikin, are those your eyes? It is so long since I saw you!"

"Mother-in-Law, these are my eyes O!"

"Ah! my pikin, is that you I'm seeing?"

"Mother-in-Law, it is me O!"

"Ah! my pikin, my own, own pikin, how are you?"

"Mother-in-Law, I am well O!"

"Ah! my pikin, how are you feeling?"

"Mother-in-Law, I feel well."

"My pikin, how do you do today?"

"Mother-in-Law, I am doing well."

"My pikin, how is my daughter?"

"Mother-in-Law, your daughter is very well."

"My pikin, how are my children?" (She meant her grand-children, of course.)

"Mother-in-Law, your children are well."

"Hummmm, my pikin, I am happy to hear that."

"Mother-in-Law, I am happy to see you looking so well."

"My pikin, won't you sit down?"

"Mother-in-Law, I just called to greet you. I cannot stay long."

So Bra Spider sat down, and Mother-in-Law — as the custom was — went to the cool clay waterpot, set in the earth floor of her pantry, and brought him a calabash bowl brimful of ice-cold water. Then she wanted to hear all the gossip of his village. Was everyone in good health? Only a healthy village can prosper and have great harvests and many children.

As the talk went on and on, Bra Spider got hungrier and hungrier. You should have seen him jumping off his little bamboo bench and skipping about the tiny room on his spindly legs. When he told of the feasts and dances in his village, he let out a hint that he was getting hungry. Mother-in-Law was glad to take the hint, for she was all ready for a guest.

She knew that whenever you prepare food you should make an extra helping for an unexpected visitor. So that morning she had prepared two big helpings of her famous *moi-moi,* and when the large red cock stood out on the porch and crowed loud and long, she knew for certain that a guest was on the way.

So she and Bra Spider sat down together to a delicious meal of porridge and *moi-moi.* The taste of the beans and palm oil in the *moi-moi* would have made anyone's mouth water. Mother-in-Law had wrapped the *moi-moi* in *olele* leaves, which gave the steamed ground beans an added flavor. Bra Spider could not have been more pleasant. All through the meal he laughed and joked. He even finished the second helping that Mother-in-Law had so carefully provided.

She too was beside herself with joy. She was not only happy to have an illustrious visitor. She was even happier that he enjoyed the food, for Bra Spider's wife also was well known for her cooking. At least Mother-in-Law was not too old to cook the same delicious dishes she had taught her daughter to make.

Although Bra Spider was enjoying himself so much, he remembered his own mother's warning: when you visit a friend, don't stay too long after the meal, for if you do you will start telling lies. Mother-in-Law had barely finished washing the plate when Bra Spider got up to leave.

"Are you getting ready to go, my pikin?" she said. "I must get you some fruits to take to my children!"

"Ah, Mother-in-Law, you are so kind!"

Before she went to the backyard to pick the fruit, she put a good amount of dried groundnuts in the hot ashes to roast. As soon as she had gone outside, Bra Spider swept up a large helping of the hot groundnuts and stuffed them into his top hat. Then he heard Mother-in-Law's footsteps and quickly clapped on the hat with the hot groundnuts right on top of his head.

But the heat was so great he could not keep his head steady. He began to shake it this way and that. He jumped here, he jumped there as the hot groundnuts roasted his head.

Here, there,
right, left,
forwards, backwards,
backwards, forwards,
left, right,
there, here!

He was still jumping and shaking when Mother-in-Law came in. "Ay! my pikin, what is wrong with you?" she cried.

"Nothing is wrong, dear Mother-in-Law, but today is Shake-head Day!"

And with that, Bra Spider shook and twisted and danced and jumped with a thousand pinpricks biting his bare skull.

"Ah, my pikin, you are ill! Was there too much pepper in the *moi-moi*?"

"No, Mother-in-Law!" squeaked Bra Spider, as the pain brought tears to his eyes. "Your *moi-moi* is the best in the world! But today is Shake-head Day!"

Off he danced again, and while Mother-in-Law packed the basket of fruit, he sang in a high thin voice:

"Mother-in-Law, today is Shake-head Day!
Mother-in-Law, today is Shake-head Day!
Mother-in-Law, today is Shake-head Day!
Mother-in-Law, today is Shake-head Day!"

He did not stop dancing when she put the basket in his hand, and then away he went, dancing through the front door and down the road.

That day Bra Spider was the finest dancer that ever was seen. All the way home he never stopped leaping and prancing on his spindly legs to the squeaky music of the Shake-head Song and the biting, burning pain of the roasted nuts on the top of his little bald head.

NOTES ON THE STORIES

Why the Baboon has a Shining Seat

The Krio people of Sierra Leone, who tell this tale, include the baboon in many of their stories, often in the role of leader. The baboon is important in stories all over the world, for it looks and acts so much like a human being.

This tale has a special meaning for us today, when we hear everywhere about the population crisis and family planning. It shows that population matters faced traditional Africa long before the coming of Western culture and Western education.

Why There is Death in the World

This is an Ibo story. Like many other African tribes, the Ibos — who live in the East Central State of Nigeria — are known for their belief in the other world, the world of spirits to which their ancestors go after death.

The Stepchild and the Fruit Trees

Child adoption is very common in Africa, and marriage to more than one wife still occurs in certain regions. In this Ibo story, however, Mazo remarried after the death of his first wife. Ijomah was ill-treated by the second wife and, as we say in Africa, Nnekeh the stepmother "took" Ijomah to mind her own children.

The mother image is very strong in Africa. When death had deprived Ijomah of her own mother's love and protection, she acquired extraordinary powers that would make up for the loss and would eventually enable her to live a comfortable life.

Ojumiri and the Giant

This tale is told among the Krios of Sierra Leone, who have their origins in the Yoruba tribe of Nigeria. The name Ojumiri comes from the Yoruba, meaning "the things (trouble) that my eyes saw." In the tale Ojumiri grew up in poverty and his family lived from hand to mouth.

Deference to elders is very important in all African communities. Ojumiri helped his mother maintain the family, was obedient to the giant's wife — and was rewarded for his obedience. Another fine quality in Ojumiri was his bravery. Even when he feared for his life, he did not give away the secret instructions of the giant's wife.

Agbado   A word meaning "corn" in Yoruba but used by the Krios to mean "snake," particularly at night

when the word "snake" should not be mentioned.

Akara	A round cake, made from rice and banana or ground beans, fried in palm or peanut oil.
Balanji	A xylophone made of strips of hard wood with hollow gourds hanging underneath as resonators. It is played with wooden hammers.
Foofoo	A paste, like very thick porridge, made from cassava that has been soaked for a few days until it ferments and then is grated.
Garri	Dry meal made by grating cassava (a root similar to a yam). *Garri* is dried over the fire in an open iron pot or on a large flat piece of steel.

Ayele and the Flowers

The people of eastern Ghana, a region that is very rich in music and dance, tell this story. Throughout Africa children are expected to consult their parents and obey them at all times, but as we see in the case of Ayele, this rule is not always followed.

"Leave it There!"

Versions of this tale, emphasizing the lesson that wisdom goes with age, appear all over Africa. I have even heard it told by Kenyans. As this story reveals, choosing a husband or a wife is a very serious matter that not only must insure the life-long happiness of the couple but also of their families. Among

some tribes it is still the custom for the wife to be chosen by the parents, and a dutiful son accepts that choice with very few questions. This has, however, been changing, and there are places in Africa today where two people may choose each other and get married.

The world of devils, like that of spirits, is a popular theme in African stories, but man usually triumphs over the super-natural beings, as Modu does in this tale.

Amala	A thick paste made from yam flour.
Arborbor	Black-eye beans, boiled and then fried in palm oil. Hot pepper and onions are added.
Eba	A paste made from *garri* (dry cassava meal).
Jollof Ress	Rice cooked in peanut oil and water with spices and condiments. Tomato paste and meat or fish may be added.
Sarra	Offerings for a sacrifice. These may be money, foodstuffs or fruits left at the crossroads.
Tero	A purple rock mined in West Africa, ground into tiny crystals, and used as eye makeup.

"Mother-in-Law, Today is Shake-head Day!"

Bra Spider's adventure is another tale told by the Krios and, like the Baboon story, the tale also has relevance to World Population Year. The Krios were probably among the first African peoples to make contact with the Western world. Their ancestors — many of them Yoruba people from Nigeria — were captured in the time of slavery and carried away to America.

When some of the slaves were eventually freed and brought back to Africa, they settled on the Guinea Coast where the Krios still live today. They named their settlement Freetown. Many became highly educated and served as teachers, preachers, and civil servants in Sierra Leone and other countries of West Africa. Because Western education deeply affected their way of living, we often find references to such foreign items as top hats and tuxedos in Krio tales.